Other I CAN READ Books by Syd Hoff

DANNY AND THE DINOSAUR

SAMMY THE SEAL

JULIUS

Story and pictures by SYD HOFF

An I CAN READ Book

HARPER & ROW, PUBLISHERS,
NEW YORK, EVANSTON, AND LONDON

JULIUS

JULIUS

Davy went to Africa.

His father was

going to catch an animal

for the circus.

"Do you want a giraffe?"

said Davy.

"No," said Mr. Smith.

8

"How about a lion?"

said Davy.

"No," said Mr. Smith.

9

"Will an elephant do?"

said Davy.

"No," said his father.

10

"I'm sorry. What we want
is a gorilla," said Mr. Smith.

11

"Some animals have

all the luck,"

said the lion, giraffe, and elephant.

12

Davy couldn't wait

to see a gorilla.

He had never seen one.

"It's time to rest,"

said Mr. Smith.

"I'm not even tired,"

said Davy.

14

Everybody took a nap.

Davy could not sleep.

Davy found a coconut.

He kicked it

into the bushes.

Someone kicked it

back to him!

"Who's in there?"

said Davy.

"I am,"

said a voice.

19

"You're a strange-looking person," said Davy.

"I am not a person,"

said the voice.

"I'm a gorilla.

My name is Julius."

They shook hands.

Davy squeezed hard.

"Ouch! You have

a strong grip,"

said the gorilla.

"Would you like to play
football?" said Davy.

"I'd love to,"
said Julius.

Davy showed Julius

how to throw a pass.

24

He showed him

how to catch one, too.

Julius tackled Davy.

"Now you tackle me,"

said Julius.

"No, thank you,"

said Davy.

27

"Look, I found a new friend,"

said Davy.

"My name is Julius,"

said Julius.

"Won't you join us for dinner?"

said Mr. Smith.

Julius had good table manners.

He knew which

fork and spoon to use.

He made no noise

when he ate his soup.

"I hear you're looking

for a gorilla, sir.

Will I do?" asked Julius.

30

"I was hoping you would ask,"

said Mr. Smith.

"Of course, we'll be

glad to have you."

31

The men carried Julius

through the woods.

Sometimes Julius

gave the men a rest.

"Good-bye,"

said all the animals.

On the ship

Julius made new friends.

35

"The food is good,
isn't it?" said a lady.
"They could give us
more bananas,"
said Julius.

"I want a fur blanket, too,"
said a man.

At last the trip was over.

"Look me up in Boston,"

said a person.

"Look me up in the circus,"

said Julius.

38

"Don't you like cars?"

said Davy.

"I'd rather swing,"

said Julius.

39

"You must be the new gorilla,"
said the circus man.
"How did you know?"
said Julius.

"We work here, too,"
said the clowns and seals.
"I'm proud to be
part of the team,"
said Julius.

41

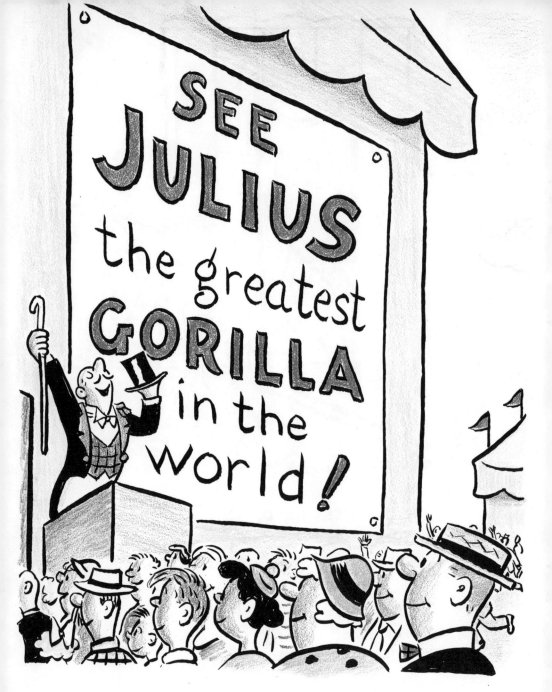

Everybody rushed to see Julius.

"He looks so strong.

I hope he can't

get out of that cage,"

said the people.

"Nobody could

get out of there," said someone.

"Why should I get out?"

said Julius.

"I like it here."

A fly came into the cage.

"I think I'll annoy

that gorilla,"

he said.

"Buzz, buzz, buzz,"
said the fly.
"Clear the runway.
I'm coming in
for a landing."

He landed on Julius' nose!

"I'll have to ask you to leave,"

said Julius.

"My nose is not an airport,"

he added. "Kindly take off."

The fly did not listen.

He stayed right there.

47

Julius shook his hand at the fly.

"Thanks for making me nice and cool,"
said the fly.

"It's so warm in here."

"I'll try scaring him,"
said Julius. He jumped up and down.

"The gorilla is

trying to get out,"

said the people.

They ran away.

"Oh, dear," said Julius.

"I scared everybody else."

"Tell them to come back,"
said the circus man.
"And don't get lost."

51

"I'll try," said Julius.

The circus people waited

and waited.

There was no sign of Julius.

"Something happened to him,"

said the seals.

"Let's go look for him,"

said the clowns.

"Do you see him?"

said the fat lady.

"I don't see anything,"

said the thin man.

"Have you seen someone
with lots and lots of hair?"
said Mr. and Mrs. Tiny.

55

"Is there anybody

in that tree besides you?"

said the giant.

"Gorillas should be easy to find,"

said the wire walker.

"Not this one,"

said the acrobats.

"Let's go to Davy's house,"

said the circus people.

"Maybe he knows

where Julius is."

Davy was playing football.

"Julius is lost,"

said the people.

"Have you seen him?"

"No," said Davy.

"But once I

kicked a coconut into the bushes

and Julius kicked it back."

"Try it again,"

said the circus people.

Davy kicked his football

into the bushes.

Someone kicked it back!

"Julius!" cried everyone.

"Oh, I'm so glad you found me.

I was lost,"

said Julius.

"Please take me back to the circus.

I love it there."

"Let's go,"

said the circus people.

The clowns got ready.

They gave Julius a mirror, too.

"We love to look at the gorilla,"

said everybody.

"I love to look at him, too,"

said Julius.